Once Upon a Babysitter:

First Time in Charge

Amber Booker

ISBN: 978-0-578-58438-6

Hi, I'm Aubrey, and today is a special day!

My mom and dad are going on a date.

So, for the first time, I am in charge of babysitting my twin brother and sister, Devin and Dakota. Hooray!

As Mom puts on her coat, she leans down to give me and my brother and sister a hug, and she says, "Aubrey, thank you for watching your brother and sister tonight! Have fun, be safe, and we love you three with all our might."

"Bye, sweetheart," Dad says, giving us a big hug, and off they went. My first night as a babysitter has officially begun!

While our mom and dad are away, I decide that the first thing we will do is play.

The twins love to play hide-and-seek. Hopefully, they remember not to peek!

We also play Devin's favorite sport, basketball, while running up and down the hall. He loves to score in the hoop. Dakota and I cheer him on as he shoots.

Twinkle twinkle,
I'm a little star

Also, we can build with blocks, creating towers, cities, and shops.

"Look, Aubrey!" Dakota says. "I can pretend this blue block is a bird and it can fly!"

Dakota raises her block high into the air, squealing in delight without a care.

"Next, I think we should finger paint," I say to my siblings. "This will be fun!"

Dakota paints a bright, beautiful star and Devin paints a picture of a car.

All of a sudden, Devin pretends he's a car! He quickly runs left, and then he turns right. During all this running, the paint takes flight.

The paint flies high in the air. When it lands, it splatters everywhere.

"I'm sorry, Aubrey," Devin says with tears on his face.

"It's okay, buddy," I say. "Can you help me clean up this place?"

The time comes to get ready for dinner.

I exclaim, "Whoever has the cleanest hands is the winner!"

My brother and sister wash their hands in the sink and then decide to sit at the dining table to have a quick drink.

Next, I turn to my brother and sister and say, "We're having spaghetti and veggies for dinner tonight."

Surprisingly, they eat all their veggies without a fight!

"Hmm, that was strange," I think to myself, but I can't complain.

The children begin to play as I clean the table and put the dishes away.

As I finish cleaning, I notice that I no longer hear the twins.

"Devin! Dakota!" I shout, but I do not hear them playing about.

The house is completely quiet, the quietest it has been all day.

So, I begin to search right away.

I search the living room and run up and down the stairs, but I don't see the twins anywhere.

Suddenly, I hear rattling from underneath the kitchen table.

"What could it be?" I wonder and walk over, as slowly as I'm able.

As I look under the table, I am caught by surprise!

The twins have gathered their favorite treats right before my eyes.

Cookies, cakes, candy, and gum.

Then, together they say, "Come join us, Aubrey! Would you like some?"

You two are so sticky," I exclaim. "Cake crumbs are all over the place! To make matters worse, you have gum on your face! You both must take a bath right away."

We rush to the bathroom, and I place them in the tub. I add extra bubble bath because that's what they love.

As I wash them clean, I notice the bubbles begin to rise.

There are so many bubbles that they cover Devin and Dakota's eyes. I say to the twins, "Maybe I added a tad too much bubble bath." It isn't a problem to them. They just giggle and laugh. They playfully pop the bubbles one by one, and I can't bear to stop their fun.

As I finish their bath, I make sure I rinse them well. They were once covered in sugar, but I couldn't even tell.

I dry them off quickly, so they won't get cold. "Please put on your night clothes," I say, and they do as they're told.

With their night clothes now on, we say our prayers
and I tuck them into their beds.

I will read them a story while they rest their heads.
First, I ask them about their favorite part of the day.
They both smile and say, "Spending time with you,
Aubrey. We love how you play."

I read their favorite story about Little Bo Peep.

As I close the book, they both fall asleep.

I tell them goodnight and gently kiss them on their cheeks.

Tonight was a great success! Spending quality time with my brother and sister was the best!

My brother and sister had fun, and I was able to be a great babysitter, a babysitter that my mom and dad trust and love.